SYBIL'S WESTERN VALENTINE

MAIL ORDER BRIDES OF FIELDER'S UNION

SUSANNAH CALLOWAY

Tica House
Publishing

Sweet Romance that Delights and Enchants!

PERSONAL WORD FROM THE AUTHOR

Dearest Readers,

Thank you so much for choosing one of my books. I am proud to be a part of the team of writers at Tica House Publishing who work joyfully to bring you stories of hope, faith, courage, and love. Your kind words and loving readership are deeply appreciated.

I would like to personally invite you to sign up for updates and to become part of our **Exclusive Reader Club**—it's completely Free to join! We'd love to welcome you!

Much love,

Susannah Calloway

VISIT HERE to Join our Reader's Club and to Receive Tica House Updates!

https://wesrom.subscribemenow.com/

CONTENTS

CHAPTER 1

The bitterly cold weather, marking the middle of winter in Fielder's Union, Arkansas, showed no signs of letting up as January spent itself out in a series of days of blinding sun. Brian Smith gritted his teeth as he pulled first one glove and then the other more securely onto his hands, stiffened by the cold. It was difficult to hold a pen in the crease of the thick leather, but after an hour in the attic of his little cabin, out of reach of the heat from the cookstove down below, he had no choice but to put the gloves back on.

Dispassionately, almost amused, he noted how much worse his handwriting got with the extra layer. Ah, well. It hadn't been first class to begin with.

He wondered if he'd ever get used to the cold here in Arkansas. The relatively balmy winter days outside of Los

Angeles, California, seemed faint and far away. Well, he supposed, they were far away – a long ways away, in fact. Forever beyond his reach, just like Rosemary…

He shook the thought away abruptly. Rosemary had gone on her merry way nearly fifteen months before, and if he knew her flighty nature, she hadn't given him a single thought since the day she informed him their engagement was off. Oh, for the three months they'd courted, he had told himself he was the luckiest man on God's green earth, to be able to capture the affection of a woman like Rosemary. She was one of nature's flitter-ers; like a butterfly, she floated effortlessly from interest to interest, making whomever she was attached to at the time feel more interesting, more handsome, more desirable. Brian, who considered himself a rough sort, was no different from the rest. And, in the end, he had been just as easy to leave behind…

And now here he was, tallying up columns of numbers as though he'd been born to it.

He sighed and pinched the bridge of his nose between his thumb and forefinger, breathing in deeply. The attic room smelled of dust – cold dust – and worn leather from the gloves and his overcoat. Outside the dirty window, the sun was beginning to go down. It would be dark soon, and he knew with a sense of dread that it meant suppertime was not far away.

Not that he didn't like suppertime; if there was one thing Brian Smith knew, his mother had always said, it was how to eat. No, it was more the prospect of sitting across from his cousin Spencer and watching how he and his wife Georgiana mooned over each other. They were newlyweds, which was bad enough, and it was almost their first anniversary, which made things much worse.

Brian didn't begrudge his cousin his newfound happiness. After all, Spencer had gone through great loss, when his first wife had died not long after the birth of their daughter. But did Spencer Frost have to be so darn loud about his happiness? Couldn't he keep it down?

Brian couldn't help but chuckle wryly at his own unreasonableness. Well, at least he knew he was being unreasonable! But his sentiments were real. Love hadn't done much of anything for him, except leave him in the dirt when he was already down. Rosemary's ghost always seemed to be standing in the corner laughing at him; or, even worse, ignoring him entirely.

If he wanted to be on time for grace, he'd better get a move on.

He stood up and winced as his bad leg took on weight; no matter how he tried, he couldn't seem to avoid the pain. With a cold gloved hand, he reached out to grasp the curved handle of the carved wooden cane, the final gift from his parents before he'd left California behind. It had replaced the crutch that had been his constant companion for three months prior to that. And now –

Now, he told himself severely, there was no point in feeling sorry for himself.

It was hard, though, when getting down the stairs seemed like a nigh impossibility.

Gritting his teeth and clenching his jaw, he made his way slowly and painstakingly to the lower floor. With his overcoat on against the frigid twilight, he closed the door of the little cabin behind him and headed for the ranch house. The home of the Frosts was well lit, with a candle or oil lamp shining from nearly every window; the Frosts liked to be cheery and bright and didn't seem to mind it might cost more. They were very different from the Smiths, that way – Allan Smith, Brian's father, had been a penny-pincher for as long as Brian could remember. Sometimes he wondered how Sadie Smith, who had once been a Frost herself, had ever ended up with a man like Allan, given the life she evidently had been raised in…

The past was past, and there was no point in speculating on it. If he spent too long thinking about marriages and how some of them lasted and some of them didn't, he would only end up getting down again. He'd spent enough time down – too much, in fact. Rosemary had worked him over, that was a fact. But it was up to him to not let her hold the reins anymore, especially since she wasn't even around. He was twenty-six, not bad to look at, and he had a decent job at a ranch – even if the job was pencil pushing and had been given to him by his sympathetic cousin.

He recognized the echoes of the pep talk he gave himself just about every night around this time, and grinned as he limped up the stairs to the front door of the ranch house. Someday, maybe it would work.

Lena Frost was the first to greet him as he stepped into the house. Spencer's six-year-old daughter had seen some changes in her life in the past year, with her father's remarriage and the fact that Leslie Brown, née Frost, had left the family home and Arkansas entirely after her own marriage. Brian's arrival not long after seemed to have made the little girl feel that a hole had been filled; she became immediately attached to her second cousin and pounced on him as he walked in the door.

"Brian! You're late for supper!"

"Lena Frost," called the girl's grandmother sternly. "How many times have I told you about leaping on your poor cousin?"

Brian grinned, wrapping his free arm around Lena and holding her close.

"It's all right, Aunt Helena. It's nice that someone's so happy to see me."

"Oh, Brian, we're all happy to see you," Helena Frost said, her brow furrowing in the concerned look that she seemed to wear so often around him. Brian knew that pity looked different on different faces. This was unmistakably how Helena Frost displayed pity. Could he help the fact that it put his back up a little?

"Don't see you rushing forward to greet me, Aunt Helena," he grumbled, but kissed her on the cheek to try and lessen the sting of his words. She put her arm through his and led him towards the kitchen.

"I'm not a six-year-old girl, Brian. Besides, if I flung myself at you the way she does, we'd both go tumbling over to the floor."

He had nothing to say to that. She was probably right, anyhow.

Rather than reply, he turned his attention to the rest of the family, who were in the process of gathering around the kitchen table. There was Uncle Teddy, the patriarch of the Frost family, with hair that matched the family name. Spencer, the only son of Helena and Teddy, was taking his seat next to his wife, smiling at her with a light in his eyes that was impossible to ignore. Georgiana, a slight, delicate young woman with exceptionally pretty features and a sweet nature, was studiously avoiding his gaze but smiling in a way that made it clear she felt it nonetheless. Brian clenched his jaw. Despite his pep talk, despite his determination not to let Rosemary's ghost sit on his shoulder any longer, he was evidently going to have to pray for patience tonight.

Why was it that his feelings were so much more raw at some times than others? Was it because it was almost a year now since he had come to Fielder's Union? Was it because he knew the Frosts were a happier family than his had ever been?

Maybe it was just because his darned leg was aching so badly in the cold.

"It looks like everything is going to plan for the dance," Georgiana was saying to Helena, evidently finishing up a conversation they'd been having previously. "I don't suppose that any of the girls in town will have trouble finding a fellow to go with."

"Considering there's one girl to every five boys in Fielder's Union, I reckon you're right," said Helena, smiling. "Imagine it – the very first St. Valentine's Day dance in our little town. And it's all because of your efforts, George."

"Goodness, no," Georgiana said, waving a hand airily. "I just happened to remember how much I enjoyed them when I was younger, that's all – and besides, everyone is always looking for an excuse to have a dance."

They fell to chatting again about the upcoming event, and Brian tried to ignore them. The last thing he wanted to hear about, when he was feeling like this, was about dancing – let alone dancing on Valentine's Day.

"Brian," his cousin greeted him, turning a fond smile on his younger counterpart. "We were beginning to wonder whether you'd make it in time for supper."

"I was finishing up the accounts for this month. Tomorrow starts February, remember."

"Sure, sure. Thank you – but I would have been sorry if it took you away from us tonight."

Brian raised an eyebrow at the comment but didn't have a chance to reply before Lena piped up, "I thought maybe you fell down the stairs. Didn't you think he maybe fell down the stairs, Pa?"

Everyone fell quiet and avoided meeting Brian's gaze; Brian himself took a moment to compose himself before he could answer his second cousin.

"I didn't fall down the stairs, Lena."

"I don't know why you insist on doing the numbers up in that drafty attic," Georgiana ventured. "It must be freezing up there, and of course those narrow stairs are a danger for anyone…"

Especially a man who might as well be one-legged, Brian filled in for her mentally.

"I don't mind it," he said, as placidly as he could.

"You could always work here, in the spare room, in the warm…"

"I need the peace and quiet."

His response, rather brusque, was enough to make her give up. He caught the glance she gave her husband, a wide-eyed look of *Well, I tried… Spencer closed his eyes briefly. What can you do with a man who won't accept any comfort or understanding?*

It gave Brian a twinge in the heart, momentarily. His cousin and his wife, in fact all of the Frost family, were trying to help him. It was his own fault if he had become so embittered by Rosemary, by the accident, by the fact that he could no longer walk without a cane – so embittered that he did not allow them to help.

Just as he was about to open his mouth and apologize, Spencer cleared his throat.

"Before we say grace," he said, glancing over at his parents, "I'd like to make a quick announcement. I don't think I can hold it in any longer."

Lena sat up straight, looking at her father with eager eyes. Brian caught the look of utter adoration that Georgiana gave her husband, and dropped his gaze to his lap, feeling ashamed.

Spencer took his wife's hand in his.

"Georgiana and I are expecting," he said. "Lena, you're going to be a big sister."

It wasn't a surprising announcement; they had been married for nearly a year, and Brian had half expected to hear that they were expecting well before this. As his aunt and uncle gave exclamations of delight and Lena leapt onto her chair to cheer – before being soundly reprimanded by her grandmother and asked to express herself in a more ladylike manner – the best he could manage was to smile at his cousin and hold out his hand for a shake.

"Congratulations," he said. "I'm very – I'm very happy for you both."

Spencer clasped his hand firmly, smiling warmly back.

"Thank you – that means a lot coming from you, Brian."

Why was that, Brian wondered – was it because his cousin knew the bitterness that plagued him, the regret over the things he had lost, how difficult it was to put a brave face on?

Or was it just the fact the two of them were family, the closest either had to a brother?

If he wasn't a bitter, loveless man, Brian thought, he could easily believe the latter. But tonight, looking around the table at his overjoyed relatives, at Georgiana smiling shyly and Spencer bursting with pride as though he'd done something that had never been done before, it was difficult. Sometimes, Brian was certain, no matter how much the Frosts tried to include him and build him up, he would never feel loved or wanted again.

As unbearable as the pain from his near useless leg was in the cold, it was nothing compared to that.

CHAPTER 2

In all of Sybil Webb's young life, she had never heard a phrase so glorious and welcome as the one she heard that day when Mrs. Patton knocked on her door.

"Letter for you, Miss Sybil."

Sybil bounded out of her chair, dropping her needlepoint heedlessly on the carpet.

"Oh, thank you, Mrs. Patton."

The older woman handed the letter over, giving Sybil a keen glance. Perhaps it wasn't expected for a lady's maid to take such liberties, but after all, Mrs. Patton had known Sybil since she was ten years old. Now nineteen and the princess of Boston's high society, Sybil wasn't about to refuse any words of wisdom from Mrs. Patton, especially since her parents were not so willing to give her the support and attention which she so desperately craved.

"This is the fourth letter this month without a sender," Mrs. Patton observed.

Sybil's heart leapt into her throat.

"Well, of course it has a sender, silly," she said, turning away toward the window and scrutinizing the cream-colored envelope. "It didn't appear by magic."

"I think you know what I mean, Miss Sybil. There's no name as to who sent it – which seems mighty unusual to me."

"Does it?"

"Just about every time you get a letter, it's got the name of the sender written large all over it, practically." Mrs. Patton snorted genteelly. "I reckon everyone in Boston is so proud to be writing to you that they want the rest of the world to hear they've got the ear of Edward Webb's favorite daughter."

Sybil turned the letter over in her hands.

"I'm my father's only daughter," she ventured.

"Oh, Miss Sybil, you know well enough what I mean." Mrs. Patton waved a hand dismissively. "Your father dotes on you, he certainly does."

"Maybe so," Sybil allowed, "but I think you had it right the first time. He dotes on his daughter – but sometimes I think he doesn't know me at all." She turned to her maid, a feeling of tension creeping into her chest, the weight of secrets about to be spilled. "Mrs. Patton, what would you say if I told you this letter…" She lifted it into the air to demonstrate, dropping her voice to a conspiratorial whisper. "This letter came from a…a man."

Mrs. Patton raised her eyebrows.

"I suppose I'd say I'd be surprised if it hadn't," she said. "The way you carry on, Miss Sybil, anyone would have to be blind not to notice it. But I don't reckon it comes from John Beauregard, all the same."

Sybil's cheeks flushed a light pink, and she lifted her head high.

"No, as a matter of fact, it doesn't. Why should it?"

Mrs. Patton folded her arms.

"I may not be society, Miss Sybil, but I reckon the whole of Boston knows your father intends for you to marry John Beauregard. I've seen him looking through the gossip columns and nodding his head whenever he sees your name attached to his." She shook her own head in obvious distaste. "Not what I call being a responsible father, but there you have it. To each their own, and maybe if I had a child of my own, I'd feel differently about it." It was clear she did not believe this to be even the slightest bit true.

Despite herself, Sybil grinned.

"Well, you're right anyhow," she said. "The letters haven't come from John. They've come from another man."

"A gentleman?" Mrs. Patton questioned sharply.

"Of course," said Sybil. "I mean – I think so."

"You think so?"

Sybil took stock of the skeptical expression her maid was now wearing and got ahold of herself.

"I know so," she said firmly. "We've been corresponding for a month, as you so ably noted, and I feel I know him as well as I know myself. His name is Henry Miller, and he's a doctor who lives in Fielder's Union, Arkansas. He's twenty-nine years old, has never been married, and was educated here in the east." She took a deep breath, feeling the tingle of nerves in the pit of her stomach, anticipating the next question to come.

"And how did you first encounter this Mr. or Doctor Miller, if I may ask, Miss Sybil?"

There it was.

"In the paper," said Sybil. "Only a page or two behind the gossip columns my father pores over so avidly. He wrote an advertisement for a Mail Order Bride – and I answered it."

For a long moment, Mrs. Patton stared at Sybil as though she had sprouted antennae.

"You've answered an…advertisement. From a stranger."

"There's no need to take that tone about it," Sybil told her swiftly. She couldn't help it; her back was up. "There are two or three matrimonial agencies here in Boston alone, on top of the Matrimonial Times."

"And how did you find out about that, Miss Sybil?"

"I saw Hettie reading it while she had her tea one day," Sybil said defensively. "I asked her about it, and she explained how it worked. There are dozens and dozens of men looking for wives out west, and there's no reason why I shouldn't consider one of them."

"Perhaps it's no reason to you," said the maid, sharply, "but it's a great deal of reason to me. Miss Sybil…" She calmed herself, but it took an obvious effort. "Miss Sybil, have you considered the fact that some man might try to take advantage of you? You're young, innocent, beautiful, and the only daughter of one of the most influential men in Boston."

"Surely a doctor in Arkansas wouldn't care about that – how could he even know about my family or where I came from?" Sybil protested. "Besides, any day now, Father is going to tell me he's arranged for my marriage to John Beauregard – and I can't marry him, Mrs. Patton, I just can't." She put a hand to her forehead, feeling a sharp pain of physical distress at the thought. Mrs. Patton watched her for a moment before sighing heavily with regret and sorrow.

Tenderly, unexpectedly, she put a hand on Sybil's arm.

"I know, dear," she said softly. "I understand. Miss Sybil, I've watched you grow up around the society your parents so cherish, and I know it is not where your heart lies. You are made of finer stuff, my dear." She paused a moment, considering her words. "What do you fear will happen, should you marry John Beauregard?"

"I'll become just like my mother," Sybil said softly. "Unhappily married to a cold man who cares more about what other people think than about my feelings. My books, my painting, all of that could be taken away at a whim. He'll want me to be just like everyone else – just like he is." She shook her head. "I can't do it, Mrs. Patton."

"I understand, Miss Sybil. I do." Mrs. Patton chewed on her lower lip for a moment, thoughtfully. "Well, what does this Doctor or Mr. Miller have to say for himself this time?"

With shaking hands, Sybil opened the envelope and took out the folded page within.

She read it over to herself silently. At her sudden exclamation of joy, Mrs. Patton lifted her head sharply.

"What is it?"

"He's decided he wants to marry me," Sybil whispered in rapture. "After only four letters, he says he's sure I'll make a fine wife." She clasped the letter to her, feeling joy surge through her heart. "Mrs. Patton, I'm engaged."

The maid narrowed her eyes thoughtfully at Sybil's proclamation but did not disagree outright.

"I understand it's customary for the girl to make a reply before it's official."

"Oh, of course, you're right. I'll write to him immediately."

A hand once again gently laid on her arm forestalled her as she turned away.

"Miss Sybil," said the maid hesitantly, "I don't want to take any happiness away from you. But are you certain this is what you want? I know you don't want to marry Mr. Beauregard – but after all, at least you've met him in person. The man who wrote this letter is a stranger to you, someone unknown. He may not be all that he represents himself to be."

Sybil shook her head.

"I know I haven't known him long," she said. "But I choose to believe him, Mrs. Patton – where would we be without belief?" She sighed happily. "Of course, I can't tell my parents. They'd forbid me from ever leaving the house again if they thought I was going to run off with a small-town doctor in the west."

"Yes, you can't tell your parents, certainly." Mrs. Patton sighed again. "Well, if you're determined that this is what you want to do…"

"I am. With all my heart."

"Then what do you propose to do about it? Tell me, and I'll do whatever I can to help you."

Sybil smiled fondly at the lady's maid. "Really?"

"Miss Sybil, having known you since you were a child, I've always thought what a great shame it was that someone like you was – well, was wasted on Boston high society."

Sybil laughed and threw her arms around the maid, hugging her tight and close. As she let her go again, it occurred to her that, though they were several years apart in age, they were rather similar in height and size.

"Mrs. Patton, did you mean it when you said you would do whatever you could to help?"

"Of course, Miss Sybil. I'm not the sort of person who opens her mouth without speaking the truth."

"Then," said Sybil, putting a finger to her lower lip pensively and eyeing her maid, "would you do me the favor of lending me a dress?"

Mrs. Patton's eyebrows shot upward.

"A dress?"

"Yes." Sybil nodded, a smile forming on her face even as a plan formed in her head. "I would like very much to borrow a dress from you, if you please, Mrs. Patton…"

The plan took another two days to come to fruition, as Sybil had to wait until the timing was exactly right. But on Sunday afternoon, her parents left her at home to go out on their society calls, accepting Sybil's excuse that she did not feel well. It wasn't entirely a lie, anyhow – she was a bundle of nerves at the idea of the action she was about to take, and the prospect of starting her new life so soon. And in such a way!

If she wasn't so nervous, she would have laughed aloud at the cleverness of it all.

The trouble was not all of the house staff were as kindly disposed to Sybil's dreams as Mrs. Patton was. In fact, she was quite sure that at least two of the other maids had let slip that Sybil had been caught perusing the Matrimonial Times; surely that was why Hettie was forbidden to read it in the house anymore. If she couldn't trust the staff, she couldn't allow them to see her leaving the house that afternoon.

She had already packed her valise, taking only a few changes of clothing and the pocket money she'd been saving up for months. It wasn't much, but it would get her to Fielder's Union. She knew where her father kept some money in reserve in his study, but she shrank back from taking any of it. It wasn't just that she was morally opposed to stealing – she also did not want to think of her parents funding her journey, whether they knew it or not. She wished her groom had sent her the money for her passage and care, but like it or not, she was to be reimbursed when she arrived.

Hopefully, the money she had was sufficient. She daren't take any.

For surely her father would find out, in the end.

She waited half an hour after her parents had left the house, to ward against any potential early return. Then she dressed herself in Mrs. Patton's spare dress, wrapped an apron around her waist, tucked her hair up under a cap, and tied her shoes with care. With her heart in her mouth, she went down the stairs, clutching the valise as though it were a lifeline.

Anna, one of the maids, was just coming through the hallway and turning into the study, a feather duster in her hand. Sybil's heart stopped momentarily, but the young woman did not even give her a second glance, going about her business and closing the door behind her.

As quickly as she dared, Sybil moved through the hall to the great double doors at the front of the house. It was a risk, as Mrs. Patton and the other servants always used the kitchen door; but she couldn't allow herself to be fully seen by the rest of the staff. The front door it was.

She didn't allow herself a breath of relief until she was out of the house, doors closed behind her, down the street, and around the corner. Then she collapsed against the brick wall behind her, feeling her heart pounding in her chest.

She had done it!

She was out of the house – and she'd made the first step toward her new life.

She took a few moments to breathe in deeply, letting her heart be calmed, before she hurried away toward her next destination. As she went, she played through what would happen in her mind – her parents returning home from their calls, elated over their inevitable success. Sybil would be called for dinner, but she would not respond. Eventually, at last, someone would ascend the stairs to her bedroom and find within the letter she had left on her pillow…

She could picture her father's eyes widening in outrage and disbelief as he read over the few words she'd left behind, telling them she was leaving town to marry a doctor in a small town in the Midwest, she would write when she was settled, and they weren't to worry…

Her parents worry over her. It made her laugh.

They wouldn't so much worry as be furious.

And when they found out where she was and what she had done, why, she wouldn't put it past her father to show up on her doorstep and demand she return home. But that didn't matter, not in the slightest. By the time her irate father arrived in Fielder's Union, Arkansas, she would be married to Henry Miller, and no one would be able to separate what God had yoked together.

Not even Edward Webb.

CHAPTER 3

The trip across the country did nothing to calm Sybil's overactive nerves. From one day to the next, she couldn't help but doubt she would ever make it to her destination. There were delays on the line; the cold, snowy weather, despite the fact it was seasonally appropriate in the first part of February, certainly didn't help matters. Nor did the illness of the conductor, due to some bad oysters, or the rumors that flew on swift wings, rumors of banditry and villainy and preying upon travelers.

It reminded Sybil briefly of what Mrs. Patton had warned her, that someone might take advantage of her position as daughter to one of the most influential men in Boston – but she pushed the thought away hastily. She had taken the precaution of traveling under an assumed name, adopting her mother's maiden name as her own surname. This, coupled with the fact that she was still wearing Mrs. Patton's rather worn and out-of-style dress, was as much protection as she could hope for under the circumstances.

Despite her misgivings and the potential for danger along the way, the train chugged and puffed into the town of Altoon on a sunny Monday afternoon, disgorging its travelers to make the change to stagecoaches for the last legs of their respective journeys. Once seated inside a rather rickety coach heading to Fielder's Union, Sybil tucked her gray dress about her knees and took in a deep breath. She had made it this far – was it possible she was going to make it all the way?

Of course, it was, she told herself stoutly. After all, she had someone waiting for her – Henry Miller, the man she was going to marry.

The thought of Henry carried her through the last part of her journey with head held high and heart full of light. Soon, she would meet him. Soon, she would be married – Mrs. Henry Miller. She would join him in his practice and help him with rolling bandages and comforting patients. And in a few years, they would have children – a boy and two girls, she pictured it. She could practically see them now.

Oh, it was all too easy to imagine her life out here, in the rolling plains of Arkansas, despite the cold and discomfort of the journey that was required to get there. It would be worth it, in the end. She was sure of it.

Fielder's Union was not a surprise, but that was only because Sybil hadn't had the faintest idea of what to expect. It was larger than she might have thought, but still far smaller than her neighborhood in Boston. In the brightness of the frigid February sun, she saw a handful of streets, lined with clapboard buildings and wooden sidewalks, the walls all whitewashed. The stagecoach rolled slowly past the local saloon, then a mercantile – a man stood outside, his head turned to the side as though he were watching for someone.

As they went by, he turned to watch, and his eyes caught Sybil's as she pressed close to the window. Something in the stranger's gaze made her stomach do flip flops. He was very handsome, in a rugged sort of way, and his gaze was direct and uncompromising. She supposed that most men in the west must look rather like him – tall, dark, wearing his hat pushed back and bearing himself with the utmost confidence. His eyes were pale in his swarthy face, the blue of the winter skies.

Suppose – just suppose – that he was actually Henry Miller.

It was unlikely. The man looked as though he ran cattle for a living. Certainly, he wasn't the doctor-ish type.

But if he did turn out to be Henry Miller – well, that would alleviate the slight but undeniable feeling of guilt that accompanied her desire to lean out of the window and watch him until he was out of sight. She'd never felt so compelled to get acquainted with a man in her life.

With determination, she put the thought of the stranger out of her mind. The stagecoach was rolling to a stop at the inn, and she had something more pressing to think about: meeting the real Henry Miller.

She wasn't sure what to expect. In his letters, he had only described himself in the vaguest terms – tall, he said, but one man's tall was another man's short. She didn't know much about men, but she knew height was rather a sore spot for those less vertically endowed by nature. He was in his late twenties, but age could be difficult to tell at the best of times. She didn't fancy staring into the face of every man who passed by, trying to determine how many decades he had seen in his lifetime.

No one who was clearly and indisputably a doctor named Henry Miller presented himself. There were a few passers-by milling about the stagecoach stop, but most of them made their decisions and either entered the inn itself or went on their way elsewhere. The thing to do, clearly, was to wait.

There was a bench near the stop, halfway between the door to the inn and the corner of the building. It was somewhat sheltered from the wind. Clutching her bag, Sybil took up her spot and waited.

And waited…

And waited…

Every now and then she dug her pocket watch out of the valise to scrutinize it. As the minutes crawled by, her heart sank further and further toward her boots. It was two o'clock now – more than half an hour after the stagecoach had arrived. And still no Henry Miller had presented himself.

As two-thirty crept ever closer, she surpassed being merely cold and began to be chilled to the bone. The sun was moving towards the horizon; as late in the season as it was, it still would get dark well before it might have in the summertime. Would she have to wait here overnight? Should she go and see about getting a room at the inn?

Fighting with the woebegone feeling that was threatening to overcome her, she opened her pocketbook and counted out how much money she had left. The results were disheartening; how much did it cost to spend a night in the inn? Perhaps she had enough. Perhaps she didn't. But even if she had enough for one night, suppose – oh, horrid thought, but suppose he didn't arrive the next day, either?

Suddenly, her exhaustion and hopelessness caught up with her and the tears she had been keeping at bay won out. She dropped her face into her hands, shoulders shaking with silent sobs – and then the sobs were not so silent. No one was around to see her or hear her...

At least, that was what she thought.

It was scarcely a moment later that she felt a hand on her arm and sat up, wide-eyed and startled.

A young woman was looking down at her, half bent at the waist, her blue eyes reflecting her concern.

"Excuse me, miss? Are you all right?"

"Oh, dear." Sybil sat up straight, wiping at her eyes. "Um – yes, yes, I'm…I'm fine."

The young woman raised an eyebrow.

"Goodness, that's hardly convincing." She seemed to reach a decision and took a seat next to Sybil on the bench. Her hand was still on her arm, offering comfort. "My name is Georgiana Frost. I haven't lived here in Fielder's Union for all that long, but something tells me you're not from around here, either."

Sybil shook her head, and gratefully took the proffered handkerchief that Georgiana held out.

"No, no – I just arrived. I've been waiting for someone."

"Just arrived on the stagecoach?"

Sybil nodded, and Georgiana glanced over toward the inn. The stage stop was empty; Sybil hadn't even noticed that it had gone again.

"That must have been well over an hour ago. You haven't been sitting here in the cold for so long?"

Sybil shrugged a little, helplessly. "I'm afraid so – something must have happened. He was going to be here to meet me…"

Georgiana Frost bit her lip, looking Sybil over as though trying to reach a decision. Abruptly, she nodded and stood up, tugging gently at Sybil's arm until she stood up alongside her.

"Come along, my dear. You need something hot to drink, and the inn is right here."

"But – but suppose it was just a mistake and suppose – suppose he shows up to collect me, and I'm not there."

Georgiana was leading her towards the inn door.

"Suppose he does. Well, he'll just have to exercise good judgement and look in the inn, won't he? Besides, if he was going to come and collect a poor visitor to this town – whoever he is – he should have had the courtesy to at least be on time."

They were through the door. Oh, the glorious warmth. Sybil could have cried again from relief. Georgiana was still leading her on, through another doorway and into a quiet dining room, where she pulled out a chair at the end of the long table and gently pushed Sybil into it. She took the seat across from her and leaned her elbows on the table, eyeing Sybil with undisguised curiosity.

"Now – Lucy will bring us some tea, won't you Lucy?" she called through the doorway. "Thank you – and you can tell me all about it. What's your name?"

As quickly as Georgiana Frost had become a guiding force in Sybil's life, it was something of a shock to realize she didn't even know Sybil's name.

"Sybil Webb." She realized too late that perhaps she should have used the name she had traveled under – but she couldn't help but trust Georgiana. And besides, what were the odds this young woman sitting across from her at the inn in Fielder's Union, Arkansas, would know anything about Edward Webb of Boston, Massachusetts, let alone his daughter?

"I've come from Boston to marry Doctor Henry Miller." She dropped her eyes to the table, waiting as Lucy brought out the tea and served them. "I expected him to be there today – we've been corresponding for a month."

Georgiana nodded gently. "And how did you meet this Doctor Henry Miller?"

"He wrote an advertisement and posted it in the newspaper."

"Ah," said Georgiana quietly. "I feared as much – my dear, let me tell you right away that I understand entirely what you are going through. I've been in Fielder's Union only a year myself, and the truth is that I was also a Mail Order Bride."

Sybil looked up swiftly, eyes wide, and her new friend nodded at her with a kind smile.

"Yes, it's true. I'll bet you thought you weren't likely to meet anyone else who has been in your situation."

"You're right about that." Sybil sat up straight, a faint smile making itself felt. She had felt drawn to Georgiana from the moment she saw her; perhaps this was why, on top of her thoughtful manner and obvious kind disposition. They shared a background.

"I've heard of others – a kitchen maid even let me read her Matrimonial Times, once. But I never expected that I would meet another Mail Order Bride as soon as I landed in Fielder's Union."

Georgiana chuckled. "And that's not all – I'm from Boston, too."

"You're pulling my leg?"

The other woman shook her head, smiling widely.

"In fact, your family name sounds somewhat familiar – is your father the Edward Webb who made such a splash in the newspapers with his investments?"

Sybil's eyes widened, but Georgiana reached out and patted her hand.

"Don't worry, Sybil – I know it may worry you, but no one will take advantage of your family or your background. Not while I'm here to watch over you." She sat back and sighed, a cloud coming over her pretty face. "On the other hand, I'm terribly afraid that your arrangements with this Doctor Miller are going to fall through."

"Oh, dear. What makes you say that?" She leaned forward anxiously. "You don't know him after all, do you?"

Georgiana shook her head regretfully.

"No – and that's what makes me worry so. Fielder's Union is a small town, and the only doctor I know of is Doctor Sanders. Now, I am rather new here, but I'm pretty sure I would have heard tell of this Doctor Miller – if he does exist."

Somehow, Sybil's heart sank even lower. Her mood had been temporarily elevated by the kindness her new friend was showing to her, but with this unexpected piece of knowledge, her hopes for the future seemed unconquerably dashed.

"But – how can that be?" she murmured. "I've received letters from him…"

Georgiana shook her head once more, looking more and more sympathetic for Sybil's troubles as the moments went by.

"It seems to me I've heard of something like this," she said. "My husband doesn't wish to gossip, especially if it might be hurtful to me – but after I had been here in Fielder's Union for a while, there were rumors of something happening in the neighboring town. A girl had been sent to marry a farmer there, but the farmer hadn't written for her at all." She sighed. "Now, it may not be like that – perhaps I'm poorly informed, and there is a Doctor Miller hidden somewhere hereabouts. But it may take some time to find out."

"What should I do?" Sybil asked, feeling as though the world had dropped out from under her feet. Georgiana, responding to her tone with sympathy, covered her hand with hers once more.

"I'll tell you what you'll do," she said firmly. "You'll come home with me and Spencer – that's my husband, Spencer Frost. We're just in town to pick up some supplies for the next week. I've got an awful lot of baking to do for the Valentine's Day dance coming up." She took a final decisive drink of her tea and then stood up, calling back to the other room. "Thank you, Lucy!"

Sybil stood. "I haven't much to pay with…"

Georgiana waved her hand dismissively.

"Never fear, my friend. Lucy's not adverse to sharing her tea now and then, and besides, Spencer's credit is good." She smiled, and Sybil could see the fond pride shining out of her eyes as she mentioned her husband. It was clear she was very much in love. That was how it was meant to be when a match was made, Sybil thought sadly, feeling her heart clench within her. But her own match was not to be – perhaps it was entirely founded on a lie.

Would she never know that kind of love?

Georgiana put her arm through Sybil's and led her back out toward the front door of the inn.

"We have a spare room at the house," she said conversationally. "It's not much, but it's free and empty, since Brian disdains to work in the big house and chooses to stick to his cold little cabin at the back."

"Brian?" Sybil asked helplessly, feeling as though she were being towed along as they left the inn behind and headed out into the coldness of the streets once more.

"Brian Smith. He's Spencer's cousin. I won't speak ill of him, especially considering you don't even know him, but I will say I wish I could understand the man a bit better. He's had a…" She broke off abruptly, biting her lip, and then shook her head and carried on. "He's had a hard time of it, poor thing. He came to us just last year and works with Spencer and his father on the ranch. Come down here, my dear. I'm sure they're at the general store – probably waiting for me if I know anything about it! I was just meeting once more with the committee to finalize plans."

"Committee?" Sybil wished to high heaven she had something intelligent to say, rather than helplessly repeating Georgiana's words, but she was feeling more and more overwhelmed by the moment. Georgiana was a force to be reckoned with.

"The Ladies' Committee for the Organization of Community Events in Fielder's Union," explained Georgiana. "Which is a long name for the four of us sitting around drinking tea and talking about parties." She laughed. "But I like it. Here we are."

She came to a stop at last in front of the general store – the mercantile Sybil had noted two hours before, when the stagecoach had gone slowly by. She wondered briefly, fleetingly, whether the strangely compelling man was still waiting around outside – but there was no one to be seen. It was unlikely, after all, she told herself. Why would he be hanging about outside the store for hours at a time?

"Ah, here they are, right on time," said Georgiana cheerfully, as the door of the mercantile opened, disgorging two men. They were both tall, and both wore hats – that was all Sybil noted about the first one before her eyes went to the second and her breath stopped.

Pale blue eyes, the blue of the winter skies above, met hers with a straightforward, questioning look.

"Sybil Webb, this is my husband, Spencer Frost," Georgiana said, tugging lightly on the sleeve of the first man. "And this is his cousin, Brian Smith."

Yes, there was no doubt about it – this was the man she had seen, however briefly, as the coach had trundled by. He was even more handsome up close, with a square jaw and a delicately-cut mouth; his sky-blue eyes were narrowed and guarded, as though he weren't quite sure what to make of her.

"Pleased to meet you, Miss Webb," said the first man politely. "Have we met her, George?"

It was the perennial question of a man who was untrained socially, delivered with the questioning glance at his wife, who shook her head with a smile.

"No, you don't know her yet, Spencer. But you soon will – I've invited her to come back to the house and stay with us."

"Ah." Spencer nodded, with a look on his face that showed vague interest but no surprise. Evidently this was not an unusual thing for his wife to decide to do, and he had no qualms with it. "I see."

"She's from Boston," Georgiana said. "And – Spencer – I think we may need your help."

She tucked her arm through her husband's and led him toward the corner, leaning up on her toes to whisper into his ear. Sybil watched them for a fleeting moment before she found her gaze being drawn back to Brian Smith. His pale blue eyes were still fixed on hers, but as she turned back to face him, they shifted, and he looked away. It was the strangest feeling – as though they had caught each other in the act of doing something secret. Her heart beat double-time, but she could think of nothing to say. Brian Smith said nothing either, lowering his head until his hat half obscured his face, keeping his eyes now on the ground.

She realized suddenly that he held something in his hand – a cane, made of some smooth dark wood, carved near the bottom with a simple design. It was an odd affectation for a man who seemed so strong and straightforward, and it was on the tip of her tongue to ask him about it before Georgiana and Spencer Frost returned.

Georgiana's husband looked worried.

"George here tells me you might need a place to stay for a few days," he said.

Sybil looked at Georgina—a few days? Did she think it would take as long as that to sort things out? And surely Henry Miller must not be around here, for Georgiana had evidently looked to her husband to know if he was. Again, her heart sank. But her new friend smiled and nodded at her encouragingly, and she took heart from that, bending to pick up her valise from where it sat at her feet.

"Yes, please – and thank you," she said. "I'm afraid I don't really know much about Fielder's Union."

Spencer chuckled.

"There's not much to know," he said. "Anyhow, you're welcome to stay with us as long as you like. Don't you worry about a thing. I'll stop in tomorrow and have a word with Tom Barnett – he's the sheriff here – and ask if he can hunt around a little, see if we can scrounge this Henry Miller up." He nodded at her and reached for her valise. "Don't worry about a thing," he repeated, kindly.

Sybil relinquished her bag to him and allowed Georgiana to link arms with her. The two men began to walk back along the wooden sidewalk, and Sybil noticed for the first time that Brian walked with a pronounced limp, favoring one leg heavily over the other. That must be the cause of the cane, of course. And perhaps that was what Georgiana was referring to when she mentioned what a hard time of it the young man had had recently.

Though he hadn't so much as spoken a word to her, Sybil's heart could not help but go out to him. Someone had shown her great kindness; she was of a strong mind to show kindness to others in return.

Especially when she couldn't seem to stop herself from staring at him.

CHAPTER 4

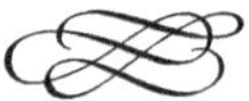

Early in the afternoon of February the eighth, Brian Smith finished the accounts for the week and slammed the dusty ledger closed, tossing his pencil on top of the large book with a sigh of relief. For some reason, the numbers had been torture this past week. Maybe it was the fact that the days had already grown warmer – unseasonably so, in fact – and he longed to spend time outside, running the cattle. If not outside, then over at the ranch house, at the very least. Something he could do, he thought with a tinge of bitterness. Like helping the women in the kitchen.

Even a year after his recovery from the accident, he was still yearning for the old days – the days that would never come again.

Sitting here stewing on it wouldn't help matters. It was just gone two o'clock, according to his pocket watch. Too early to head over for supper, but maybe Georgiana would make him some tea.

Or maybe someone else would take pity on him…

He stopped the thought dead in his tracks. In the week since Sybil Webb had arrived in Fielder's Union and taken up temporary residence in the spare room of the ranch house, she had steadily infiltrated Brian's thoughts, day by day, little by little. He couldn't understand it. Sure, she was pretty, but pretty girls were a dime a dozen – at least, that was what he wanted to believe, though, in fact, he couldn't think of too many that were actually living there in Fielder's Union at the moment. Before Sybil Webb arrived, he would have said his cousin's wife Georgiana was the prettiest girl in the county, let alone the town. Now, however…well, if he allowed himself to think about it, he might come up with a different answer.

So he was determined not to think about it.

Still, Sybil's presence wouldn't deter him from going up and seeing what he could cadge from the kitchen at the ranch house. He stumped down the stairs from the attic, pulled on his leather coat, decided it was too warm for it, took it off again, dithered about the way his shirt collar was lying, and retied his shoes – all the while railing at himself for thinking so much about what he looked like. He never would have given such a thing a second thought, just a short week ago…

It must be something about the fresh air and sunlight, he decided as he made the short trek over to the house. It was getting into his blood, under his skin.

Nothing to do with Sybil Webb at all.

Nonetheless, despite his protestations, when he stepped into the kitchen at the big house, his eyes were drawn immediately to her. She sat with the other girls at the big kitchen table, bright head bent over her task. The table was littered with stacks of paper, paste pots, pencils, ink pens, and small jars of paint. It befuddled him.

"What on earth…"

Lena looked up, her eyes taking on a familiar, fond shine.

"Brian! You're too early for supper."

Brian chuckled as she leapt from her chair and wrapped her arms around him.

"Lena, I don't just come here for food, you know. You make me sound like a mercenary."

"Maybe that's not what you're here for, but I reckon you wouldn't turn some down," Helena said, smiling at him as she stood up from the table. "Take a seat and I'll get you some tea."

"Oh, I'll get it, Helena." Georgiana started to stand as well, but her mother-in-law swiftly put a hand on her shoulder.

"No, dear, I think you'd better stay seated."

Brian noted that Georgiana nodded gratefully and sank back down, a slightly green tinge to her face. Evidently her condition was beginning to get to her. He wondered if anyone had mentioned it to Sybil yet. Of course, that wasn't the kind of thing that was often discussed with strangers – but he couldn't quite bring himself to think of Sybil as a stranger.

That was pretty strange, itself.

Again, he brushed the thought away like an irritating gnat. Obediently, he took a seat at the table, directly across from Sybil – it was the only available seat, he reminded himself – and Helena sat a plate of cookies in front of him.

"Try these on for size," she said. "It's a new recipe, from Mrs. Hendershot in town. She swears by 'em, but we're not yet convinced whether they're good enough for the Valentine's Day Dance."

Brian thought momentarily about passing them up on the moral grounds that he didn't hold with such nonsense as Valentine's Day, or dancing – but cookies were cookies, after all. He bit into one and nodded his thanks as his aunt set a mug of tea down beside him.

"That what all of this is? Something to do with the dance?"

"These are secret admirer cards," Lena told him with the air of a learned instructor, as she cut out a misshapen heart from a piece of paper. "At the dance, everyone can use them to send love notes to the person they love."

Brian laughed; he couldn't help it. Lena was so earnest, so matter of fact.

She was too young to know any different, anyhow.

"Is that what your ma told you?"

Her stepmother was getting up from the table again, a hand on her middle.

"I don't know where she heard about it, but I think it's a wonderful idea. The world needs more love notes, in my opinion." She gasped a little and her face went pale. "Excuse me a moment…"

Helena, brow furrowed in concern, followed her out of the room, leaving Brian, Lena, and Sybil, who had still said nothing but was concentrating on the card she was putting together.

"There," said Lena with satisfaction, folding the heart in two and handing it to Brian. "Now open it, and you'll see what I mean."

He opened it. Inside, there was a roughly drawn stick portrait of a man in a hat, with a figure that he had to assume was a horse just behind it – or maybe a dog. On the other side, a smaller stick figure with long hair was smiling at him.

"Is this you and me, Little Lena?"

"Yes," she said, grinning at him. "It's my love note to you because I love you. You can keep that one." She handed him another heart. "And you can use this one to send me a love note, too."

Brian smiled. It was impossible not to love the little girl; her enthusiasm was so genuine, so real, even though she really didn't know him very well. Though they were related, he'd only come into her life a short time before. It touched his heart.

"All right," he said. "This will be the only love note I send, Lena, so I hope you like it."

Sybil glanced up at him, and he caught a smile. Wordlessly, he smiled back, and their gazes stayed fixed on each other for just a few seconds longer than they might have otherwise. Suddenly, he felt his heart start up much faster than it usually would.

That was all he needed, he reckoned. A bum leg and heart trouble to boot.

"Mind passing me that pencil near you?"

Sybil took up the pencil and reached across the table to hand it to him. As he took it from her, his eyes were still fixed on hers; he hadn't intended to touch her, but his grasp overshot and his fingers slipped down along hers, almost like a caress, before he took the pencil from her. Her eyes dropped immediately, and Brian wondered why he was so breathless all of a sudden, as though he'd been running.

He hadn't felt like that in a very long time.

"Thank you," he managed.

"You're quite welcome."

It took a few moments for Brian to regain his composure. All the while, he wished desperately that Helena and Georgiana would return – at the same time, he found himself wishing exactly the opposite. May they stay away for days. Years, even. And may Lena find a reason to vacate the room, too. If he could have a few moments alone with Sybil – well, what would he do about it? Nothing, he told himself firmly. He would do nothing because he felt nothing. He was just having a mild heart attack, that was all.

"Say, where's that accent from?" he blurted out.

Sybil smiled but didn't look up at him. "I suppose it's from the same place I'm from."

"And where's that? Back east, I guess."

"Boston, Massachusetts."

"Huh. Not Boston, Pennsylvania, eh?" He grinned. "Well, I reckon that's why it sounds a little familiar. You talk kind of like Georgiana does."

"Yes, we do both originate from Boston," Sybil said, now frowning in apparent concentration at the paper in her hands. "Entirely different neighborhoods, however."

"I guess you two didn't grow up together."

"No, we did not."

"Hmm. Funny how you both ended up here from matrimonial agencies, though." He glanced at Lena, but she wasn't paying him the slightest attention. She was now drawing a love note for someone else -- the name inside the little heart appeared to be "Caleb," which Brian assumed must be Caleb Ormasher, the eight-year-old boy who lived just down the road. He shook his head. Young love – well, better that it stay that way, instead of plaguing people when they got older. He certainly had given up on it for himself.

"Guess that's just a coincidence."

"Indeed."

"How do your parents feel about you coming out here, away from them and everyone you know?" he ventured. "I can guess it might be mighty hard for a loving mother and father to see their daughter go off to marry a stranger. Even harder when it turns out that the stranger may not even really exist."

This got her full attention. She lifted her eyes to him and paused for a moment, considering her words.

"The truth is," she said, hesitantly, "I haven't told them where I am…and I haven't really even told them what I'm doing."

Brian raised his eyebrows. "You're pulling my leg."

"No." A firm head shake accompanied the negative. "I haven't even told Georgiana this yet, but – when I left the house, I left a note behind. That's all."

"Huh." Brian stared at her, trying to wrap his brain around why a girl would do such a thing. It seemed wildly out of character – but then again, he didn't know her so well, did he? None of them did. It just felt like they did – felt like they had known her practically forever. But she was an outsider to this house. Just like he was, except even more so because she wasn't even related…

His feeling of kinship to this girl, of being drawn to her, became even stronger even as he contemplated the fact that he neither knew nor completely understood her.

One thing was certain, however – whatever she had done, there must have been a good reason for it. She certainly didn't seem the type to act without thinking.

But neither did her gaze or tone invite further questions. Perhaps if Lena had not been there, he would have ventured to ask more regardless. But Lena was there, and so instead he contented himself with saying, "Well, you're here now. If I was someone's father, I'd want to know at least where they were – and that they were all right." He smiled at her, and after a moment, she smiled back. "Even if I wasn't invited to come and visit."

It seemed that he had said the right thing, for her tense face relaxed further and she nodded, reaching for another piece of paper.

"Perhaps I'll send them a love note," she murmured, and the sly smile that accompanied this told Brian that she did, after all, have a sense of humor. He relaxed in return and bent his head to the valentine Lena had given him to write on, beginning to sketch a drawing for the little girl – a kitchen table, and three happy stick figures sitting around with pencils in their spindly hands, all smiling.

CHAPTER 5

On February the eleventh, Sybil finally got up her courage enough to ask about Brian.

She didn't ask Brian about Brian, of course – her courage would never be so great as to manage a feat like that. But Georgiana, who was seated across from her with her head bent over her sewing, having recovered from another bad bout of morning sickness only a little while before, seemed a much more manageable target.

Sybil put down the mending that she had been entrusted with.

"What happened to Brian?"

Georgiana glanced up at her, but did not stop her tiny, neat stitches.

"Which part are you referring to? His broken leg, or his broken heart?" She sighed and lifted the piece of cloth to examine it more closely. "Or his broken mind."

The frankness of her friend took her aback. Sybil thought through her options. She had thought of Brian's peculiarities as being one and the same, rather than three separate problems. Of course, there was the fact that he had rather a bad limp and had to use a cane – but his sarcasm, his wry sense of humor, his occasionally negative attitude, she had simply viewed as part and parcel of who he was. Was it possible he hadn't always been that way?

She shied away from the thought of pressing Georgiana on Brian's heart. Already, more than once, the thought had crossed her mind that the young man seemed to hold his cousin's wife in rather high esteem. But that was just her imagination, surely. And besides, she couldn't begin to fathom she might be jealous over a harmless little infatuation with a cousin-by-marriage…

She caught herself there, stopping the thought as hastily as possible. She wasn't jealous at all. She had nothing to be jealous of. She had no right to be jealous. She wasn't even certain why the word had come to mind.

Besides, she was probably imagining things.

Asking about Brian's limp, on the whole, seemed like her safest route.

"Will you tell me about what happened to his leg?" she asked meekly. "Or will he be upset we're discussing it?"

"Oh, I reckon he might be," said Georgiana airily. "Bless his heart, he does seem to get upset about quite a lot, doesn't he? But that's all part of the brokenness." She eyed Sybil closely, as though she were a tricky series of stitches. "Are you certain you want to hear?"

Sybil hesitated but nodded.

"Can I take it, then, that you're not...how shall I put this... un-interested in my husband's cousin?"

A wild blush crept across Sybil's cheeks before she could catch it. She let go of her mending and clapped her hands over her face.

"I don't know that I would put it like that, precisely," she managed, struggling to maintain her composure. "Only – well, I do rather like him. He's very likable."

Georgiana laughed.

"I'm not sure everyone would agree with you on that – in fact, Brian can be singularly sour when he isn't putting himself out to be otherwise. But perhaps he has a reason. You see, it's been a year since the accident happened, but time has not yet healed that wound. He was a ranch hand for a large horse ranch in California – had been working there for a few years, from what I understand. At nearly twenty-five, he decided he was going to settle down there and start a family. He courted a young woman named Rosemary, the daughter of the owner of the ranch – everyone thought she would ignore or disdain his advances, but he won her over, I suppose, with the charm that he can, occasionally possess… when he wants to."

She sighed. "She was a flighty girl, and Spencer says it surprised everyone when she agreed to marry him. Even Brian, I suppose."

"She sounds as though she might not have been good for him," ventured Sybil, though she was arguing with herself over the surge of undeniable jealousy that came up into her heart, and what she really wanted to say was 'She might not have been good enough for him.'

"That's as may be – I can't say I disagree with you, though I never met the girl. Well, just a few months after they were engaged, there was a terrible accident. Another ranch hand needed help with a wild horse that was unbroken and getting loose, and Brian rode in to help. The stallion kicked Brian's horse, and of course the poor thing kicked back. Brian was thrown from the saddle and caught in the middle of two very furious beasts." She shook her head. "On the whole, it was a miracle he survived at all, let alone in as good a shape as he did."

Sybil stared at her friend, feeling the horror of the accident wash over her. "How awful."

"Yes." Georgiana nodded, her face tight and pensive with sympathy for her cousin. "It was terrible – and it didn't stop there. He didn't wake up for four days, and they thought that he might never recover. But he finally woke – and then he began to get better.

"It wasn't until a few weeks later that the doctor told him finally that the broken bones in his leg were too badly crushed to ever entirely heal. He would never ride as a ranch hand again." She shook her head. "It wasn't until then, when he was at his lowest, that this Rosemary, his bride to be, decided she had had enough of waiting around for her man to heal, and told him that the engagement was off. She didn't even have an excuse, to hear Spencer tell it – for, of course, Brian won't talk about it – she simply lost interest in him."

"Oh, that's terrible."

Georgiana sighed once more and picked up her sewing again.

"I never knew him before all this happened," she said. "But Spencer said he remembers clearly when they were younger and spent time together – he says Brian has changed greatly, and he's certain it's because of what happened to him. It's bad enough to feel you've lost your livelihood and your ability to walk and run over a tragic accident, something that occurred because you were trying to help a friend. But it must be so much worse to lose the woman you love because of something that wasn't your fault.

"Brian's physical recovery took more than three months – after he could stand and walk again, Spencer wrote to him and asked him to take over the books here at the ranch. I'm glad he wasn't too proud to accept; he needed the work, of course, but it can be difficult for a man to swallow his pride and allow others to help him, even if they are family. As for Brian's mental and emotional recovery – well, he's stubborn as all get out, and I'm afraid the girl who left him has damaged him more deeply than any of us will ever know. But he won't talk about it, other than to sneer when we speak about romance or love, or to glare at Spencer and me when we smile at each other." She sighed. "It's been rather difficult, to be honest with you."

Hearing this from Georgiana put so much of what Sybil had observed in an entirely new light. Yes, she had noted that Brian seemed to dislike it when Georgiana and Spencer were too "newlywed-ish"… but she had put it down to her suspicion that Brian had rather a crush on his cousin's wife. That was what jealousy did, whether it was unfounded or not, she chastised herself. It made you see things that weren't even there and miss things that were.

"Well," Georgiana said briskly, folding up her sewing and putting it in the basket at her side. "Now that you know about Brian, what do you think of him?"

"I think," said Sybil slowly, poking at her own feelings as though to make them come out into the open, "that he is a very badly damaged young man – and my heart goes out to him even more." She looked up at her friend. "He told me I should write to my parents."

"Yes?"

"Because he thought they would be worried, not knowing where I was."

Georgina tilted her head curiously. "Indeed…"

"He's not an unsympathetic man," Sybil said, trying to explain. "He thought of others – he doesn't even know them. He doesn't really know me. But he was concerned about their pain, their worry." She sighed. "I think there's more to Brian than meets the eye. And if he has been broken, well – perhaps he just needs time to heal."

Georgiana smiled and patted Sybil's hand.

"Perhaps," she said. "Time – and a little female attention wouldn't hurt, either."

Her friend left the room, leaving Sybil to sit by herself and think over what she'd heard. It all made sense now, Brian's bitterness interspersed with his sudden outpourings of kindness, empathy, concern…the way he delighted in Lena, showering the little girl with attention, as though she were safe. Someone that he could dote upon without worrying she would turn on him or reject him.

The thought occurred to her that perhaps that was how her father had felt, when Sybil herself was a little girl.

She had written to her parents the very day Brian had suggested she do so. The letter may have arrived in Boston by now. She couldn't help but wonder whether she would receive any reply – she had told them most of the truth, that she had come to Fielder's Union to marry a doctor named Henry Miller. The fact that Henry Miller had so far failed to turn up, she did not choose to mention.

The fact that she grew less and less disappointed about that with every passing day…well, she didn't mention that, either.

CHAPTER 6

Spencer frowned so deeply that his brow furrowed in three separate trenches. Brian put a hand on his cousin's shoulder.

"Don't give yourself a headache."

"I'm just trying to wrap my brain around this, that's all." Spencer scratched his forehead. "Numbers have never been my strong suit."

"I know. That's why you called me in, isn't it?" Brian sat back in his chair and sighed. "Among other reasons, like pity."

Spencer glanced at him, narrow-eyed, but didn't pick up on the bait. It was a conversation they'd had multiple times in the year that Brian had been in Fielder's Union. It never failed to develop into an argument.

"What it looks like you're telling me is that somehow, beyond all reason, we actually made a profit over the winter season so far."

"Let's not get ahead of ourselves," Brian cautioned him. "It's only mid-February. Still plenty of time to lose money like usual."

Spencer stared at him for a moment and then threw his head back and laughed. He clapped him on the shoulder.

"Well, I don't know how you did it," he said, "but I think hiring you to keep track of the books was the best decision I've ever made."

Brian grinned as he folded the ledgers shut once more and returned them to their place on one side of his little desk.

"No, the best decision you ever made was marrying Georgiana. Did you taste that pie she made last night? I thought I'd died and gone to heaven."

"George is much more than just the food she makes, you know, Brian."

"I know, I know."

"Girls aren't just put on this earth to bake you pies."

"Please, spare me the lecture," Brian said, waving a hand. He was only half joking. This was another conversation he'd had with his cousin more than once, and it usually went even worse than the first kind.

"For instance," Spencer said, leaning back on the desk and folding his arms, "I can't help but notice that, despite her lack of pie-baking ability, you and Miss Sybil seem to be getting on pretty well."

Brian raised an eyebrow at his cousin. "You would prefer I fight with her?"

"No, that's not what I'm saying, and you know it. I'm saying…" Spencer shrugged. He wasn't the sort of man who was comfortable with this type of conversation, and the fact that Brian was staring him down certainly didn't help the situation any. "Maybe it's time to move on from Rosemary."

Brian's eye twitched a little at the unexpected mention of her name, but he was surprised to find that the surge of bitterness he usually experienced at the thought of her simply failed to appear. Why was that? He felt strangely bereft. Where had it gone? He'd worked hard at that bitterness, at cultivating and keeping it…

It made him feel vulnerable, and he lowered his gaze to the desk before them, reaching out to take up his pencil and roll it between his fingers, anxious to have something to do.

"I…" he said and had to pause and clear his throat before the following words would emerge. "I like Sybil. She's a nice girl. Just as nice as Georgiana, which makes me think that those Boston matrimonial agencies know what they're doing."

"Sure," said Spencer encouragingly.

"But here's the problem with Sybil and her niceness," Brian said, dropping the pencil abruptly. "She can be as kind as she wants, to someone she feels sorry for – but that doesn't mean she'd take me seriously as a suitor."

Spencer stared at him. "You're not serious."

"I'm dead serious." And for once, he was. He wasn't trying to pass this off as a joke or whitewashing it with a thick layer of sarcasm. He wasn't even doubting his cousin's pure motives, for nothing but unselfishness would ever cause Spencer to intentionally bring up a subject as awkward as this.

"A man who can't even walk properly, who relies on a cane to stand up straight – a girl like Sybil needs better." He paused. "She deserves better."

Spencer was quiet for a moment, shaking his head.

"And that's why…"

"Wait," Spencer broke in, holding a hand up to stop his cousin. "Let me tell you something, before you go making excuses as to why you can't expect Sybil to behave like a reasonable, decent human being. When Georgiana came here, I made a terrible decision. I decided to mistrust her reasons for being here."

He hesitated a moment. "I wasn't…entirely wrong in doing so. Leslie…well, Les made a decision she didn't have the right to make, let's put it that way. But she only did it because I had forced her into an impossible position. I was trying to hold her back from love, from marrying Matthew, because I wanted her to take care of Lena. And when Georgiana came here, even after I realized how I was so drawn to her, I still rejected the idea – I didn't want anyone to make decisions for me. I didn't want anyone to tell me what to do. And I didn't want…"

He stopped, and Brian realized suddenly that his breathing was ragged. What was going on in his cousin's mind? It looked as though he were about to break down in tears.

"I didn't want to let go of Lorraine," Spencer finished. "It felt dishonest. I'd had a chance at love and lost her. Why should I get a second chance? I was never good enough to deserve it." He leaned forward and put a hand on Brian's shoulder. "That's just it," he told him, voice low and steady. "You'll never be good enough to deserve your second chance. But sometimes you get one anyway. And only an absolute fool would turn down a gift like that."

He squeezed Brian's shoulder meaningfully, and then turned and went down the stairs, leaving Brian on his own in the attic. For a long moment, Brian sat there and pondered over just what his cousin might have meant. The lost Lorraine – Spencer's first wife, Lena's mother – had devastated Spencer when she had died. That much, he knew. But as to how Georgiana had come to Fielder's Union, and why Spencer had almost rejected her entirely, well – he didn't know that. He didn't know any of it.

And he felt…left out.

But it wasn't their fault. They knew everything about him, about his past.

It *was* his fault. He had separated himself from the Frost family, told himself they only suffered his presence out of pity, made himself feel as though he were an outsider. His own fault.

My own fault.

For the first time, it occurred to him that perhaps the Frosts had been trying to make him feel welcome, not because they were sorry for him, but because they genuinely loved him. Because they were family…

It was a difficult realization to come to, far more difficult than the unexplained absence of his habitual bitterness.

Brian looked out the window at the clear skies. Unseasonably sunny, unseasonably warm – as though spring had come early to Fielder's Union, and as though the middle of February was as full of warmth as the hearts of the Frost family were full of love.

He was still pondering over this series of revelations the next day as he waited in the sitting room for the family to descend from their preparations for the dance.

Leaning one elbow on the mantel above the fire, which was settling into embers for the evening, he murmured, "How did I get pulled into this?"

"It's just a dance," came the voice from behind him. "Not torture."

Brian spun around to see a vision before him. Not just any vision – a vision in blue satin, with her hair piled high on top of her head, long gloves pulled up to her elbows, delicate hands interlaced before her. She tilted her head to one side, smiling whimsically at him as he searched for something to say.

When the words came out, of course they weren't at all what he was really thinking. "Dancing is torture," he said. "For some people."

Sybil adjusted her gloves, affecting an air of unconcern. "Are you telling me that you don't like dancing, Brian Smith? You needn't be so dramatic about it."

He didn't like the thought of dancing – but he had to admit to himself he liked her, very much. Standing there in front of him, she was the most beautiful thing he'd ever seen.

His denial, his bitterness, his anger all suddenly seemed as though they were very, very far away. The strongest emotion he felt in the moment was regret; regret that, with his cane, he wouldn't be doing any dancing with this beautiful girl.

The girl he'd once thought of as merely pretty, perhaps worthy of being compared to Georgiana. What a fool. He could pity himself, for once, rather than letting others do it for him.

But if he couldn't dance with her, at least he could offer her his arm to lead her out to the buggy outside.

He took a deep breath and stepped forward. Without waiting for him to lift his arm in invitation, she slipped her arm through the crook of his and gave him a cheerful smile.

"I think," she said, "despite everything, that you're going to have a very good time."

Though he was not a habitually optimistic person, and though the idea of watching her dance with other men all evening should have been classified as torture, Brian Smith still had a feeling she was right.

CHAPTER 7

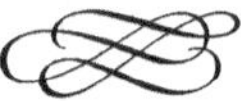

The denizens of Fielder's Union were in a rare state. It wasn't unusual for the town to have a shindig, a get-together, maybe even the occasional picnic. Christmas time was a popular opportunity for everyone to put on their finery and preen. But today, Valentine's Day of 1888, Fielder's Union's best and brightest weren't just preening.

They shone.

It wasn't just the people, of course. The entire town hall had been decked out almost beyond belief. As Sybil stepped inside, her arm still through Brian's arm, she shook her head in wonder.

"Georgiana, I don't know how you managed this. It's beautiful."

"Sure is," said Spencer, tugging his blushing wife a little closer to his side and smiling widely at her. She wriggled in his grasp until she was loose and reached for Lena's hand.

"It wasn't just me, of course," she said, though the compliments were obviously a pleasure to her. "It was the committee."

"The Ladies' Committee for Listening to Georgiana Frost's Good Ideas and then Sharing the Credit," Brian murmured in a voice that was just loud enough for only Sybil to hear. She threw back her head and laughed.

"Come on – I see punch on that table over there."

She led him eagerly through the thronging crowd, taking care not to move too quickly lest he stumble. Still, his cane tripped up more than one person as they went, though when she looked back, he was smiling, and she couldn't help but suspect that he might have done it on purpose.

As they poured their glasses of punch, the music started up. There was a string band in the corner on a dais; though they were small, they were lively, and the townsfolk let out a cheer and took their places for the first dance.

Sybil leaned back against the wall next to Brian, feeling utterly content just to watch them for the moment.

Brian nudged her.

"Don't let my sorry self stop you from dancing every tune. I won't feel badly if you leave me behind."

Sybil chewed on her lower lip, eyeing him. "You say that, Brian, but somehow I can't escape the feeling that you mean precisely the opposite."

His sky-blue eyes met hers, and for a long moment, the two sized each other up. At last, Brian chose honesty over flippancy, and sighed, leaning forward to speak quietly to her.

"You want to know the truth, Miss Sybil?" he said. "I didn't want to come here tonight. I didn't want to come when I first heard about it, two months ago, and I didn't want to come even more once I met you. Because as much as this simply isn't fun for me to be here with a crowd of people I don't know, drinking bad punch and pretending to be staggered over the decorations – the worst thing I could imagine is having to sit here and watch while you dance with every man here but one. Me."

Her heart skipped a few beats, she was sure of it – and then it rose until it seemed to float somewhere near the wreath-bedecked rafters. She stepped back and looked him in the eyes.

"Well, then," she said, "why don't you do something about it?"

He tilted his head curiously, and she took his hand.

"Be the one man I do dance with," she told him. "What's stopping you?"

Brian raised his eyebrows. "You're joking."

She shook her head.

"I reckon maybe you're too pure-hearted to notice," he said, lifting his cane, "but I have a constant companion here who might have something to say about that."

Sybil fixed her gaze on his once more and spoke slowly.

"Brian Smith," she said, "I may not have known you long, and I may not know you well, but one thing I do know. You're too stubborn to let anything stand in the way of doing what you really want to do. All you have to do is put your mind to it."

His eyes dropped before hers. "You really believe that?"

She smiled at him. "With all my heart."

He wasn't the most graceful dancing partner she'd ever had, that much was certain. But even as they moved slowly around the dance floor, with a few mumbled apologies slipping from between his lips as they went, her heart was still floating on wings far above them, and she wasn't sure it would ever come back down.

She didn't mind that in the least, either.

As glad as she was that Brian didn't resist her efforts to get him to dance, she was almost equally glad when he took her up on her tactful suggestion that perhaps one dance at a time would be best for both of them, rather than dancing the night away. Regaining his grip on his cane, he led her toward the far corner, away from the majority of the crowd and into relative quiet. As they went, he was fumbling in his pocket.

"I've got something to give to you, Sybil," he began abruptly. "And I know it isn't much – but it's what I've got. So."

He opened his hand between them. In his palm was a pink paper heart, folded in half.

Sybil exclaimed in delight. "Don't tell me I have a secret admirer!"

Brian grinned at her. "An admirer, anyhow. After tonight, I don't care who knows it."

She took the paper and opened it, smiling warmly at the simple sketch within.

"Brian, you're more of an artist than I would have expected for someone who handles the ranch accounts."

He waved a hand carelessly. "Numbers, drawing, it's all just moving a pencil on a piece of paper."

Sybil examined the sketch more closely. It was clearly a scene she was familiar with – the kitchen at the ranch house, detailed minutely. At the table before the roaring fire, three figures: a man, a woman, and a little girl.

"It's the three of us, making these cards. You, me, and Lena."

"You're right," he said, grinning – though a bit bashfully, she was delighted to note.

"Oh, but Brian," she said, folding the paper and handing it back to him, determined despite the momentary doubt and alarm that rose in his eyes. "You promised Lena that you would give this back to her. She gave it to you specifically for that purpose."

"Well…" he said, frowning. "Can't a guy change his mind?"

Firmly and regretfully, Sybil shook her head.

"You have to give it to Lena, or you'll break her heart. It doesn't belong to you anymore – it belongs to her."

"I don't want to break that little girl's heart," he said slowly, thinking it over. "I guess you're right – if it doesn't belong to me to give, I'll have to give you something else instead… another heart."

She quirked an eyebrow at him, half expecting him to pull another love note from his pocket.

"Which heart is this, if I may ask?"

Brian took her hand and held it carefully. After a moment, he pressed a kiss to her open palm.

"The only one that I have to give," he said. "Mine."

Her own heart seemed to stutter to a stop. For a moment she stared wildly at him. Then the reality of what he was saying rushed in on her like a warm breeze in the summertime, belying the cold of the February night outdoors.

"Do you mean it?"

"Miss Sybil," said Brian wryly, "I think one thing you'll learn pretty quick is that I never say things I don't mean."

Despite the fact there were so many in the town hall, so many who may have been watching them curiously in speculation, she didn't pull away when he leaned down and brushed the lightest of kisses on her lips. Indeed, she had to will herself not to follow after him when he stopped.

"Whoever would have imagined," she murmured, "that when I came here to marry a small-town doctor, I would find myself in love with a…with an…accountant instead!"

Brian tilted his head curiously.

"Are you sorry?" he asked quietly.

"Sorry about what?"

"That you never met your doctor – your Henry Miller."

Sybil couldn't help but chuckle.

"Sometimes, Brian, I think that Henry Miller was a clever trick that the good Lord played in order to introduce me to you. How else could you explain the two of us?" She laced her fingers through his. "No, I'm not sorry. I'm not sorry at all."

Brian Smith nodded, a smile of satisfaction taking up residence on his handsome features.

"Good," he said.

CHAPTER 8

On the day after St. Valentine's – a day that would live with a bright flame in her heart forever, Sybil was certain of it – she awoke with the sun. Given that it was still the middle of February, this mean that the sun rose rather late, and she had overslept.

When she tumbled downstairs, haphazard, and out of breath, she was greeted by Helena, who took one look at her and laughed.

"I had a feeling all of that dancing last night would go right to your head," said the older woman cheerfully. "I believe you enjoyed yourself more than any other person there, and that's saying something." She pulled out a chair and set down a cup of coffee. "Come on, my girl, sit."

Gratefully, Sybil slid into the chair and took a deep swig of the hot, dark brew.

"It takes one to know one," she managed once it had restored her ability to speak. "I'm certain I saw you and Mr. Frost out there, dancing the night away."

Helena chuckled.

"Oh, Teddy and I still can out-dance many of the youngsters, that's true," she said. "In a town like Fielder's Union, it's hard to pass up a chance to kick up your heels, especially after a hard winter." She sat down across from Sybil and leaned forward. "Poor Georgiana is feeling ill again this morning – she didn't get up too much sooner than you, but I put her right back in bed again. Lena's up there with her, tending to her step-ma." She took a sip of her own coffee, her eyes fixed on Sybil. "The boys are out in the barn, of course, where they always are this time of day. So it's just the two of us, Miss Sybil. You and me."

Sybil felt a twinge of nervousness in the pit of her stomach.

"Yes," she said guardedly. She liked Helena, as she liked all of the Frost family, but the way that the older woman was going about this made her doubt what the outcome of this conversation might be.

Helena cleared her throat delicately.

"I couldn't help but notice – well, no one could, I'll be bound – that you and my nephew seemed to particularly enjoy each other's company." She paused and raised an eyebrow as though waiting for Sybil to speak. Sybil said nothing, but she could feel a hot blush well on its way and coming at a running pace. "Has he spoken to you about his intentions? His feelings?"

"Well, I," said Sybil, and had to stop to get control of herself. How had it been left the evening before? After the sweet kiss he had given her – one which evidently Helena had not seen, or she would undoubtedly have led with that – she had mentioned that she was in love with him. Oh, so casually. And he had, oh so casually, certainly implied that the feeling was mutual. But nothing had been said – nothing solid. There was no engagement. And Brian hadn't given her any real idea as to what his intentions were.

The realization of this, coming on the heels of her elation after the night before, made her heart sink to her toes. But it was too soon to doubt him, she told herself.

…was it not also, possibly, too soon to trust him?

"Well, not…exactly," she managed. "That is, we certainly…he definitely…"

There was no certainly, and there was no definitely, she realized. There was only what he had told her – that he was giving her his heart. That wasn't nothing, but was it *enough?*

Enough, from a man who was obviously well known for his bitter and cynical attitude toward life, and especially toward love?

Seeing her obvious discomfort, Helena Frost kindly reached out and put a hand over the younger girl's.

"Never you mind," she said. "I think I know what you mean to say. My nephew is a good man, Sybil, but he's a complicated one. And he's been wounded in the past, as I'm sure you know. Well, there's world enough and time for him to make his stand and say his piece. I would be mighty surprised if he never gets around to it; he's a determined man, too, and once he decides he wants something, he sets out to get it."

That was quite a reputation to have, Sybil reflected. And it made sense, with what she had been told about his past. When he had set out to catch Rosemary, the daughter of his boss, for example – everyone had thought she would overlook him. But he had pressed on, persevered, determined…and had won out in the end.

Except, of course, that he hadn't. Rosemary had left him.

It was no wonder, really, that he had been so bitter about love. But if she had the chance, if he gave her the chance – she swallowed hard at the thought that he might not, after everything – then she would try to prove differently to him.

If only he would give her the chance.

"Well," said Helena, taking a final sip of her tea and standing up, "I reckon one thing you ought to do is write to the matrimonial agencies in Boston and let them know that you were sent here under false pretenses. Maybe this imaginary Doctor Henry Miller won't try to pull the same trick again, but it seems to me he could have done it more than once, and if there's a way to help any other girls avoid the same heartache, that's the right thing to do."

"Of course," Sybil murmured thoughtfully. "We wouldn't want anyone else to…endure the same heartache…"

It was difficult, suddenly, to remember that a few short weeks ago she had been devastated by the fact Henry Miller hadn't shown up to greet her at the stagecoach stop. How naïve she had been, how young.

She glanced up at Helena.

"I don't suppose you've heard anything else from the sheriff about who might have written that advertisement?"

Helena shook her head.

"Sounds like he ran dry on the investigation," she said. "It's hard to pinpoint letters down when the return address is a lie, after all. And no one at the post office here remembers anyone sending a letter to the newspaper in Boston." She bent to glance out the window. "Although, as a matter of fact, if you're keen on asking the sheriff, you can do so yourself. He just walked up to the veranda."

"Really?" Sybil frowned, puzzled. "That's unusual, isn't it? This early in the day…"

"I reckon so, but there he is, nonetheless. And it looks as though he's got someone with him."

"The someone doesn't look as though he's a small-town doctor, does he?" Sybil inquired wryly. Helena chuckled.

"No, he doesn't. He's no small town anything, as far as I can tell. I'd say he's got big city written all over him."

A tiny, irrational dart of fear lodged itself in Sybil's heart.

"What…what makes you say that?"

"His suit," said Helena, with a shrug. "The way he carries himself. And the sheriff keeps glancing sidelong at him, as though he's not quite sure…Yes, I'd wager he's a businessman, no doubt, and Sheriff Barnett doesn't know what to make of him." She put down the cloth she was using to wipe out her teacup. "Well, he's about to knock on the door, so suppose we just go and solve the mystery?"

Clearly expecting Sybil to follow her, she left the kitchen.

For a moment, Sybil sat frozen. She was trying desperately to give herself a pep talk, to help herself to see clearly beyond the fear, but it didn't seem to be working.

It couldn't possibly be…

He wouldn't have come all this way, would he?

Yes, she knew. Yes, he would. Once he found out where she was, he would undoubtedly be on his way, determined to regain his daughter.

His property…

She swallowed past the lump that appeared in her throat. At the edge of the table, she saw a piece of paper, colored brightly pink, that had slipped into the cracks between the smooth-polished planks that made up the surface. With a careful fingernail, she levered it out and smoothed it before her. A small, forgotten heart from the other day, left behind and forlorn.

She folded it in two and held it tightly in her fist.

With a feeling of dread in her heart and her steps dragging, she forced herself to stand up and walk toward the front door. Helena had opened it by now and was talking easily to the sheriff, who was an unassuming man with a friendly manner. Next to him stood the man who had big city written all over him, the businessman who no one knew what to do with, the one who caused the lawman to side-eye him.

There was no more room for doubt – or for hope.

Her father had finally found her.

CHAPTER 9

It was Lena who came running for Brian, leaping through the scrubby plants that were left in the aftermath of the winter season, calling at the top of her voice.

"Brian! Brian!"

He heard her all the way up in the attic. A spark of fear shot through him – had something gone wrong? Was someone sick? Sybil? Georgiana and the baby?

He was halfway down the stairs when Lena burst through the door, and nearly fell as he tried to gain some dignity in front of the little girl. Lena had no use for dignity, and no patience for his cane; she flew up the stairs and tugged at him, trying to get him down all the more quickly.

"What is it? What is it, Lena, what's wrong?"

"It's Miss Sybil," the girl panted, eyes wide.

Brian groaned. His worst fear, he was afraid, was about to come true. "Is she ill? Has she hurt herself?"

Lena shook her head.

"Come quick," was all she said.

'Come quick' was all well and good for Lena to demand of him, but Brian's ability to deliver was severely limited. Cane in hand, he hobbled as quickly as he could in Lena's wake, making his way to the veranda at his top speed. But before he even arrived at the steps, he could see the problem. There was a man standing there alongside the sheriff – a man Brian didn't know, but whose identity he could easily guess.

Sybil stood just outside the door, a shawl wrapped around her shoulders, her arms folded and head down. She looked… defeated. He had never seen her look that way, and it made his heart ache. He never wanted to see her look like that again.

"Brian," she said softly. "My father, Edward Webb."

The man was sleek and starkly handsome; it was easy to see where his daughter had gotten her looks. But the look he turned on Brian was anything but appealing.

"Brian who?" he said rudely. "Not Doctor Brian Henry Miller, I assume."

"No," said Sybil. "Brian Smith. He lives here on the ranch. His uncle is the owner."

Edward Webb made a dismissive gesture with one hand.

"If he isn't this Doctor Henry Smith, I don't care to speak to him," he said. "I needn't talk to anyone except this man you claim you are engaged to marry."

"I told you, Father…"

Her voice broke and Brian could see she was very near to tears. He stepped forward, catching a look of disgust from Edward Webb as the businessman caught sight of his cane.

"Sybil," he said, gently, "it's going to be all right. Everything is going to be all right."

"I demand an explanation for all of this," Webb said to the sheriff next to him, who heaved a sigh as though he had already discussed this exact thing many times over. "I demand to know where this Henry Miller is."

"And I told you, Mr. Webb, we don't know that Henry Miller ever really existed."

"So my daughter is not engaged," said Webb triumphantly, as though he had just won a major battle. "In which case, she must come back with me."

Sheriff Barnett lifted his hands. "Mr. Webb, that might be how things are back east, but here in Fielder's Union…"

"I don't care about your union, Sheriff. I'm the girl's father. She told me she was coming here to be married. I arrive here, to ensure she's being cared for, and there's no husband in sight. Not even a fiancé." He snorted loudly, as though this were beyond belief. "I don't know how she managed to be taken by something like this, but I think anyone would agree with me that she should return to her home and her family – instead of relying on the dubious kindness of strangers and law enforcement that can't even tell her whether her contract of marriage was ever valid to begin with."

"Now, hold on a minute," the sheriff began hotly, but Brian stepped forward again, reaching out to Sybil.

"She isn't here with strangers," he said, putting a hand on her arm. "She's here with us."

"Oh, yes? And who exactly are you?"

For a long moment, the two men stared each other down, eye to eye. Edward Webb's hands were clenched into fists at his sides, Brian saw; his own hands came to rest gently on top of his cane. If the other man decided to take a sudden swing at him, there was no chance that he'd be able to dodge or deflect it.

But if Edward Webb wanted a fight, then by golly Brian would give him one.

On the thought, he glanced over to Sybil. Her pretty face wore an expression of extreme distress; an expression which

Brian did not understand at first. She had left her father behind already. She had made her decision. He had no legal right to demand she return with him; she was a grown woman, not a child, and she had a home. She was cared for…

He took another look at the tears that stood in her eyes and suddenly understanding dawned on him.

Yes, she knew her father could not enforce her return. But her own feelings might…

He remembered how she had spoken of her parents, shortly after they had met. There was no doubt that, despite the feelings that had led her to run away in the first place, she still longed for them to be a part of her life. She wanted their love, their attention. That was what any daughter would want.

He glanced sideways at Lena, who looked up at her newest friend with the devotion and adoration that any daughter would give to a beloved mother. Lena was so fortunate; though she had lost her birth mother, she had been granted many others. Her grandmother Helena, her stepmother Georgiana, and now…and now, Sybil.

Sybil did not want to go back to Boston. He knew it as surely, as solidly, as he knew his own name. But neither did she want to fight with her father. She didn't want to close the door that might one day lead to a good relationship with her parents.

And so, Brian could not fight on her behalf, either.

This flood of realization crashed over him in a split second, and as he turned back to the older man, he saw the question forming again on his lips.

Who exactly are you?

Brian lifted his head proudly.

"I'm Brian Smith," he said, "and I'm going to marry your daughter."

The reactions ranged across the board from all present. Edward Webb, predictably, scowled. Helena gasped in delight. Lena clapped her hands and cheered.

And Sybil turned to him with eyes full of wonder.

"You are?" she murmured quietly.

He smiled at her swiftly.

"I am," he said, just as quietly, and then turned his attention back to her father. "Mr. Webb, it's true the man Sybil intended to marry has not presented himself. But the more fool him, in my opinion. I may not have known your daughter for very long, but we are certainly no strangers, which should soothe your concern about that, at least. I'm not a doctor, either, but I do have a job and I can – and will – provide for her. She'll lack nothing, Mr. Webb, especially not love."

He reached out and took Sybil's hand. "The fact is, for a long time now I haven't believed in love. Well, I knew it existed for some people. But it didn't exist for me – any more than Henry Miller exists for Sybil." He chuckled wryly. "At least, that's what I thought. Sybil taught me otherwise. And now that I know – I'm not going to let her go, Mr. Webb, unless she chooses to."

He glanced back at the pretty face of the girl standing next to him. "If your worry is that she won't have a home and family here, someone to care for her, a husband – that's no concern, not anymore. But if she would rather go back to Boston, and chooses not to take me up on my offer of marriage…"

"You know what my answer will be," Sybil murmured.

Brian grinned. "I'd still like to hear you say it out loud."

With her other hand, she took his hand from hers and turned it palm up. Then she set something in the middle of it, something she had been carrying the whole while. It was small and folded and meant nothing to anyone looking on – except to Brian, who knew what it was the moment he saw it.

Sybil smiled up at him.

"I've given you my heart," she said. "It's mine to give – and now it's yours."

Hardly daring to believe what was happening, Brian closed his hand tightly over the folded paper heart. He met her gaze, and the rest of the world fell away from them. There was nothing now apart from the two of them – and that was all he needed.

"Is that a yes?"

Sybil laughed. "You're awful pushy," she said fondly, and drew him closer to her. "It's a *yes*."

The End

CONTINUE READING …

Thank you for reading ***Sybil's Western Valentine!*** Are you wondering **what to read next?** Why not read ***The Handsome Boarder?* Here's a peek for you:**

In horrified shock, Jael Wheeler stared, hardly comprehending what a sobbing Mrs. Jenkins was trying to tell her. "But," she stammered, "he should be home any minute now."

"You poor child." Mrs. Jenkins wept harder, taking Jael into her arms, holding her close to her bosom. "I'm so sorry, so very sorry."

Mrs. Jenkins lived three brownstone houses down, and Jael had known the woman all her life. More people, some Jael knew and some she didn't, fidgeted in an uneasy cluster close by. Men dragged their hats from their heads, the late evening's darkness partially hiding their expressions.

"I don't understand," Jael continued, baffled and frightened. "What happened?"

A uniformed police officer stepped closer to the door, his cap in his hand. "It was an accident, miss. The horse, well, it spooked. Took off. Your father, I'm sorry, your father died almost instantly."

"He's dead?"

"Yes, miss. The horse and the buggy ran right over him."

Mrs. Jenkins straightened, wiping her face with a kerchief she dragged from her dress pocket. "Jael, honey, you shouldn't be alone. Not after this. You come stay with me. We'll be glad to have you."

"He's *dead?*"

Jael fought to gain understanding in the midst of her shock. Her father had been killed. Run down as he walked home from his excursion to the gambling hall. The same place he went nearly every night, regardless of weather or their current finances. Vaguely, Jael wondered if he'd won at cards for once.

"Jael? You're too white. Are you going to faint?"

"I – I –"

She swayed on her feet, forcing both Mrs. Jenkins and the officer to seize her arms. Disbelief spread through her, a faint hope that they'd come to the wrong house seeped into her mind. "Are you – can you be sure it's – him?"

Mrs. Jenkins burst into wails, her kerchief to her mouth. "I saw him, honey. Your father is dead."

From that moment, events blurred in Jael's memory. She recalled Mrs. Jenkins taking her down the street to her own townhouse, a comfortable place with thick rugs on the floors, oil paintings on the walls, her kind and compassionate husband giving Jael a hug.

Visit HERE To Read More!

https://ticahousepublishing.com/mail-order-brides.html

MORE MAIL ORDER BRIDE ROMANCES FOR YOU!

We love clean, sweet, adventurous Mail Order Bride Romances and have a lovely library of Susannah Calloway titles just for you!

Box Sets — A Wonderful Bargain for You!

https://ticahousepublishing.com/bargains-mob-box-sets.html

Or enjoy Susannah's single titles. You're sure to find many favorites! (Remember all of them can be downloaded FREE with Kindle Unlimited!)

Sweet Mail Order Bride Romances!

https://ticahousepublishing.com/mail-order-brides.html

ABOUT THE AUTHOR

Susannah has always been intrigued with the Western movement - prairie days, mail-order brides, the gold rush, frontier life! As a writer, she's excited to combine her love of story with her love of all that is Western. Presently, Susannah lives in Wyoming with her hubby and their three amazing children.

www.ticahousepublishing.com
contact@ticahousepublishing.com